3 3052 01332 9778

D0624847

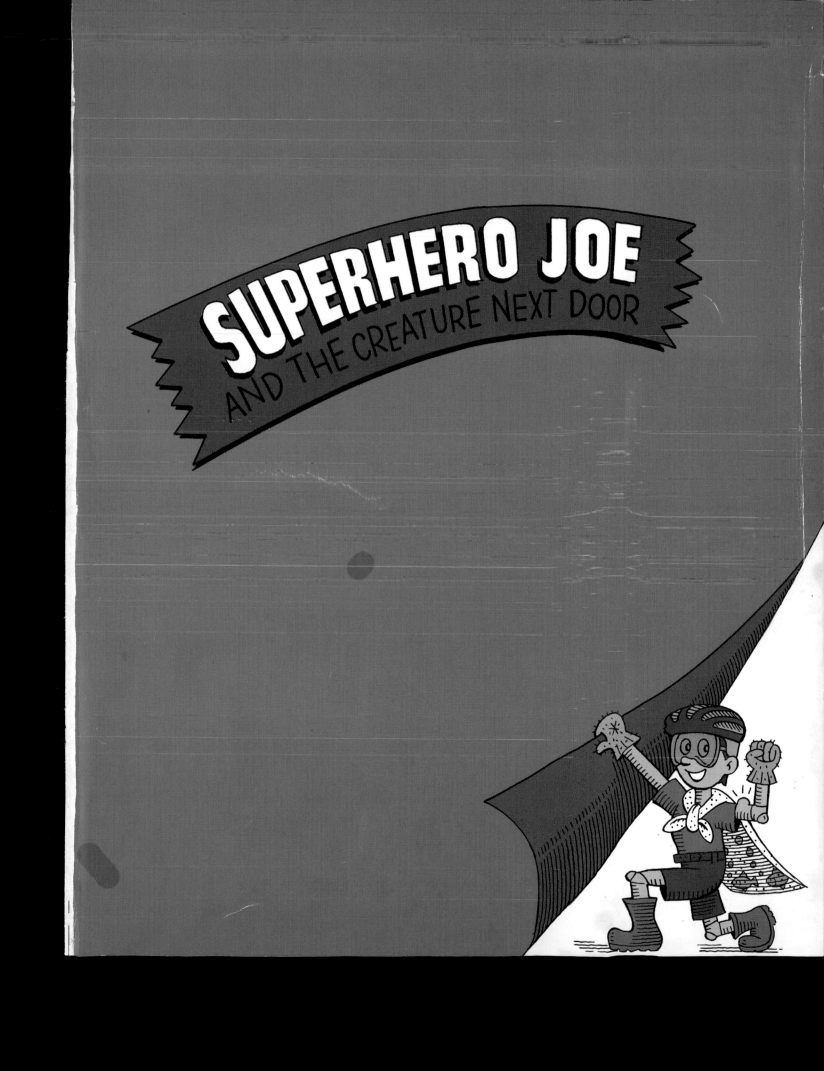

WRITTEN BY JACQUELINE PREISS WEITZMAN
DRAWN BY RON BARRETT

A PAULA WISEMAN BOOK
Simon & Schuster Books
for Young Readers
New York · London
Toronto · Sydney
New Delhi

SUPERHERO

FOR LARRY, MY LIFELONG SIDEKICK—J. P. W.

SIMON & SCHUSTER BOOKS FOR YOUNG READERS
AN IMPRINT OF SIMON & SCHUSTER CHILDREN'S PUBLISHING DIVISION
1230 AVENUE OF THE AMERICAS, NEW YORK, NEW YORK 10020
TEXT COPYRIGHT © 2013 BY JACQUELINE PREISS WEITZMAN
ILLUSTRATIONS COPYRIGHT © 2013 BY RONALD BARRETT
ALL RIGHTS RESERVED, INCLUDING THE RIGHT OF REPRODUCTION
IN WHOLE OR IN PART IN ANY FORM.
SIMON & SCHUSTER BOOKS FOR YOUNG READERS IS A
TRADEMARK OF SIMON & SCHUSTER, INC.
FOR INFORMATION ABOUT SPECIAL DISCOUNTS FOR BULK PURCHASES, PLEASE
CONTACT SIMON & SCHUSTER SPECIAL SALES AT 1-866-506-1949 OR
BUSINESS@SIMONANDSCHUSTER.COM.
THE SIMON & SCHUSTER SPEAKERS BUREAU CAN BRING
AUTHORS TO YOUR LIVE EVENT. FOR MORE INFORMATION OR TO BOOK AN EVENT,
CONTACT THE SIMON & SCHUSTER SPEAKERS BUREAU AT 1-866-248-3049
OR VISIT OUR WEBSITE AT WWW.SIMONSPEAKERS.COM.
THE TEXT FOR THIS BOOK IS HAND LETTERED.
THE ILLUSTRATIONS FOR THIS BOOK ARE RENDERED IN INK
AND COLORED DIGITALLY.
THANKS TO PAUL COLIN FOR HIS KEEN JUDGMENT AND DIGITAL EXPERTISE.
MANUFACTURED IN CHINA
MANF CODE 0613SCP
2 4 6 8 10 9 7 5 3 1
LIBRARY OF CONGRESS CATALOGING-IN-PUBLICATION DATA
WEITZMAN, JACQUELINE PREISS.
SUPERHERO JOE AND THE CREATURE NEXT DOOR / JACQUELINE PREISS WEITZMAN ;
ILLUSTRATED BY RON BARRETT. – 1ST ED.
P. CM.
"A PAULA WISEMAN BOOK."
SUMMARY: JOE CONQUERS HIS FEAR OF THE STRANGE CREATURE MOVING INTO THE
HOUSE NEXT DOOR, AS WELL AS THE TREE HOUSE IN THE CREATURE'S BACKYARD.
ISBN 978-1-4424-1268-2 (HARDCOVER) – ISBN 978-1-4424-5075-2 (EBOOK)
[1. SUPERHEROES–FICTION. 2. NEIGHBORS–FICTION. 3. TREE HOUSES–FICTION.
4. MOVING, HOUSEHOLD–FICTION. 5. IMAGINATION–FICTION. 6. FEAR–FICTION.]
I. BARRETT, RON, ILL. II. TITLE.
PZ7.W4481843SVC 2013
[E]–DC23
2012023608

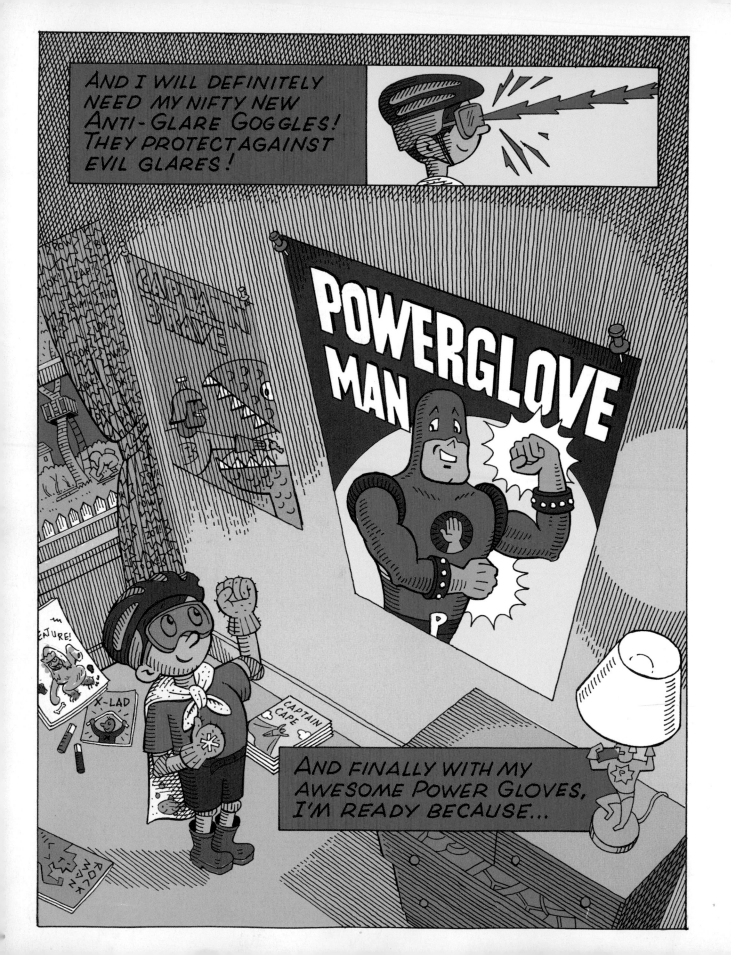